KU-049-864

Nermal has never been Garfield's favourite kitten. But with a bulldog on the prowl, Garfield is forced to come to the rescue...

Acknowledgments
Background artwork and design by Gaynor Berry.
Storyline by L. McColm.

A catalogue record for this book is available from the British Library.

First edition

Published by Ladybird Books Ltd Loughborough Leicestershire UK
Ladybird Books Inc Auburn Maine 04210 USA

Copyright © 1991 United Feature Syndicate Inc.
© LADYBIRD BOOKS LTD MCMXCI
Printed in England (3)

GARFIELD
the hero

MUNCH!
GOBBLE!
SMACK!

Based on the characters
created by JIM DAVIS

Ladybird Books

Garfield poked his nose out from underneath his blanket. Was that coffee he could smell? Coffee meant it was time for breakfast, and Garfield never missed out on food, however sleepy he was.

In fact food was the only thing that could get him out of bed. So he yawned, stretched, and padded his way across to his food bowl.

But what was this? All that was in the bowl was a tiny piece of lettuce, with a big hairy caterpillar staring up at him.

"I hope this is a dream," thought Garfield.

"I've put you on a diet," said Jon, Garfield's owner. "You're too fat!"

Garfield was horrified. Food was his love, his life, everything!

FAT!

6

Surely he hadn't put on *that* much weight?

But what could he do?
There was only one
thing for it – revenge!

Shredding a few
curtains should change
Jon's mind fairly quickly…

Perhaps even more fun than that, he could eat everything that was in Jon's fridge. Then *Jon* would have to go on a diet!

Before Garfield could do anything, there was a miaow from the kitchen table. He looked up and there was a kitten, sitting next to Jon. It was Nermal.

"Just think, Garfield," said Jon, "if you lost weight you might be as cute as Nermal."

"I'd rather eat a caterpillar," thought Garfield. He didn't like Nermal very much. When he came to stay Jon always played with Nermal and never talked to *him*. Garfield was jealous. Now Jon was giving Nermal his own breakfast.

That was the last straw! Garfield stomped off to his favourite armchair to sleep.

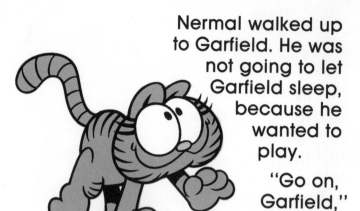

Nermal walked up to Garfield. He was not going to let Garfield sleep, because he wanted to play.

"Go on, Garfield," said Jon. "Why don't you go and play with Nermal?"

This had to be a Monday morning, thought Garfield. Everything always went wrong on Mondays.

There must be some
way out of this.

The only things that
Garfield enjoyed
doing were eating
and sleeping. The
last thing he wanted
to do was play
with Nermal.

Then he had
an idea. This
should keep
Nermal quiet for
a while, he
thought.

Garfield looked down at Nermal. "Come on," he said. "Let's go and play in the garden."

"That sounds fun," thought Nermal and followed Garfield to the door.

"After you," smiled Garfield.

"This is strange," thought Nermal. Garfield was not usually this nice to him. But everything seemed all right, so he walked out through the door.

Garfield grinned. His plan had worked. He swung his foot back and slammed the door shut.

That should keep Nermal out of the way for a while.

Nermal sat down outside and glared through the door at Garfield.

SCRATCH   SCRATCH

He thought it was really unfair of Garfield to do this to him. After all he couldn't help it if everybody loved him.

It started
to pour with rain.

Garfield didn't feel at
all sorry for Nermal. He
thought it served him
right, and he settled
down to sleep.

Outside, Nermal shivered. He looked round the garden and what he saw gave him a fright.

Standing by the front gate was the biggest bulldog the kitten had ever seen – and the gate was open!

Nermal miaowed, but that turned out to be a mistake.

The bulldog heard him and began to stomp into the garden.

Nermal started to scratch at the front door again. Perhaps Garfield would hear him and let him in. Surely he wasn't *all* bad.

But Garfield was sound asleep.

Then Garfield stretched and yawned. What was that noise?

He looked through the door and saw the bulldog walking towards Nermal.

Garfield panicked. If anything happened to Nermal, he would really be in trouble. Jon might never give him pizza or lasagne ever again!

Garfield leapt at the door handle, hoping against hope. If he could get the door open, he might just be able to save Nermal. But no matter how hard he tried, the door stayed closed.

"Maybe Jon could help," thought Garfield. He ran over to Jon's chair, but Jon couldn't understand that something was wrong.

Hey, Jon!?

"What's up with you now?" asked Jon. He was puzzled. It was not like Garfield to jump up and down like this.

22

Now Garfield was very worried indeed. The bulldog was getting nearer and nearer to Nermal, and Jon wasn't doing anything. Then Jon noticed the kitten wasn't around.

"Where's Nermal?" he asked. Sagging with relief, Garfield pointed towards the door. Jon looked and saw the bulldog.

"Nermal!" cried Jon, horrified.

Jon rushed to the door as fast as he could. He opened it and managed to grab Nermal just in time.

The bulldog growled and tried to get in, but Garfield shut the door in his face.

Suddenly Jon realised what Garfield had done.

"Garfield, you've saved Nermal's life!" said Jon. "You're a hero!"

Garfield felt proud. He had never been a hero before, but perhaps he could get used to it.

"I think we should have a party," said Jon.

A party! Garfield was really happy now. Parties meant food, and after all the excitement he was very hungry!

"I'll cook pizzas and lasagne for everyone," declared Jon.

Garfield stuffed his tummy with pizza and lasagne.

"Thanks for saving me from that nasty bulldog," said Nermal.

"Don't mention it," replied Garfield. "Besides, I saved myself from something even worse."

"What's that?" asked Nermal.

"A nasty diet!"

MUNCH!
GOBBLE!
SMACK!